DENISE LEWIS PATRICK

RED DANCING SHOES

paintings by

JAMES E. RANSOME

TAMBOURINE BOOKS  NEW YORK

To Mama Ida, Grandma Lillian, and Muh Dear, with
thanks for their special grandmothers' love
D.L.P.

In memory of Rosa Lee Williams
J.E.R.

Grateful acknowledgment is made for permission
to reprint the following copyrighted material.

Text copyright © 1993 by Denise Lewis Patrick
Illustrations copyright © 1993 by James E. Ransome

Tambourine Books, a division of William Morrow & Company, Inc.,
1350 Avenue of the Americas, New York, New York 10019.
Printed in Hong Kong by South China Printing Company (1988) Ltd.
Book design by Golda Laurens

Library of Congress Cataloging in Publication Data

Patrick, Denise Lewis. Red dancing shoes/by Denise Lewis Patrick:
paintings by James E. Ransome.—1st ed. p. cm.
   Summary: Delighted with her shiny new red shoes, a little girl
dances through town to show them off to everyone she knows.
   [1. Shoes—Fiction. 2. Dancing—Fiction.] I. Ransome, James E., ill. II. Title.
PZ7.P2747Re 1993 [E]—dc20 91-32666 CIP AC
   ISBN 0-688-10392-8 (trade).—ISBN 0-688-10393-6 (lib. bdg.)

The illustrations consist of oil paintings which were
scanner separated and reproduced in full color.
10 9 8 7 6 5 4 3 2
First edition

ISBN 0-669-36507-6

2 3 4 5 6 7 8 9 10 -WB- 00 99 98 97 96 95

Grandmama went on a trip.
And when she came back,
she brought everyone presents.

Daddy got a tie.

Mama got a yellow blouse.

Big Sister got a necklace.

But my present was the most special.
It was a pair of the finest, reddest, shiniest shoes
that anyone had ever seen.
"Thank you, Grandmama," I whispered.
"They're dancing shoes!" Grandmama told me.
"Why don't you try them out?" she said.
So I did.

I did the Twist.
I did the Swim.
Big Sister let me wear her dancing skirt
so I could spin around and around.

Those shoes felt wonderful.
They didn't even squeeze my toes.
I loved my new red dancing shoes.

Big Sister guessed just what I was thinking.
"If you want to show off your shoes," she said,
"come to the store with me."
Big Sister walked out the door. I danced.
Then I stopped and peeked down at my feet.
My red dancing shoes smiled up at me!

Before I knew it, those shoes had danced me along the road to Miss
Josephine's garden. "Miss Josephine, look!" I shouted. "See what
Grandmama brought me?"

"My, my," said Miss Josephine, rising up from her knees. "Those
are the reddest shoes I have ever seen. I believe they are redder than
my roses."

She clipped off one of her biggest, reddest roses and gave it to me.
My red dancing shoes *were* redder than her roses. Big Sister helped
me put the rose into my hair.

Then my red dancing shoes pranced and danced me past the library
and past Mr. Ky Frazier's dry cleaners, right up through the
big screen door of the grocery store.
"That's some fancy footwork there, girl!" Miss Eva said.
"New shoes?" asked Mr. Tony, leaning over the counter.
"They're my dancing shoes," I told them. "Watch me."
I did the Mashed Potato.
And I did the Jerk.

I felt a little hot, so Big Sister asked for two grape snow cones.

Miss Eva piled crunchy ice into the paper cups.

Then she poured juicy purple syrup all over the ice.

I bit into my snow cone very carefully.

I didn't want to drop a bit of gooey syrup on my shoes.

Big Sister and I started home.

"Can we stop at Nen's?" I asked. "I want to show her my dancing shoes."

Nen is Grandmama's sister. She's my favorite aunt. She always lets me swing in the big wooden swing on her front porch.

We turned the corner. I could see Nen sitting in her swing. I wanted her to see my red dancing shoes *now*. Suddenly those shoes started running. I was running too.

"Nen! Look!" I shouted.

"Be careful," Big Sister said.

But just as Nen looked up at me, I tripped on a rock. My snow cone flew into the air, splashing ice and purple juicy stuff everywhere. "WOOF!" I fell onto the dusty path, making a smoky brown cloud all around me.

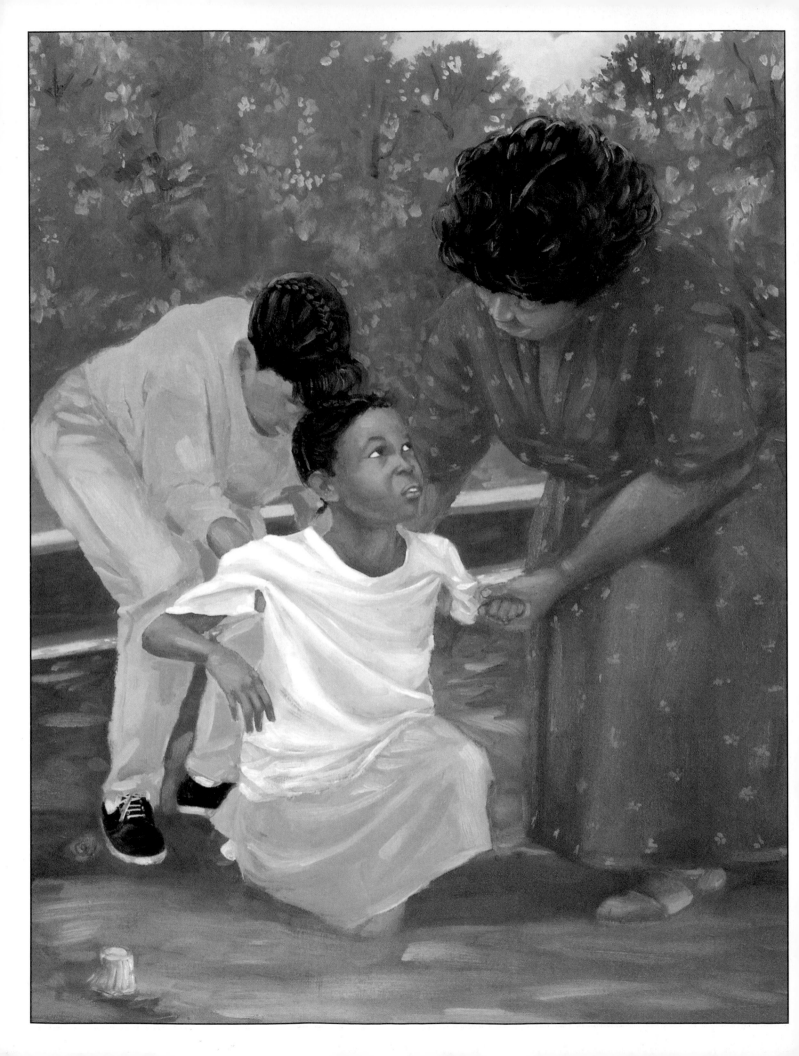

Nen was off the swing in a second, picking me up. Big Sister was dusting off my clothes. But I looked down at my feet. The beautiful, shiny, wonderful, red dancing shoes were sticky and blotchy and muddy.

"M-My dancing shoes!" I cried. I couldn't take my eyes off my shoes. They didn't look new anymore. They didn't look pretty anymore. I bet they couldn't even dance anymore.

"Let's sit down," Nen said. She went inside and brought us glasses of cool lemonade. "Do you feel better?" she asked.

"No," I said.

"I see you have pretty new shoes," she said.

"Not anymore," I said.

"Those are her dancing shoes," said Big Sister.

"I can't dance in them now," I told Nen.

"Are you sure?" she asked me.

I turned my toes in.

Then I turned my toes out.

My littlest toes started feeling funny.

"It's not the same," I sighed.

"They used to be shiny and red and new."

"Let's go into the kitchen," Nen said.

She took my hand and smiled her secret smile. Then she sat me on a chair and unbuckled my shoes. She took a cloth and ran some water over it.

Next she slipped her hand into one of my shoes, right where my foot ought to be. With one big wipe, she cleaned the mud and blotches right off. She opened a cabinet and took out a jar.

"But that looks sticky," I frowned.

Nen took another clean cloth and dipped it into the gummy mess inside the jar. She patted the cloth onto my shoes. "Now put them on," she told me.

Nen pulled one of my feet onto her lap. Then she held the cloth tight and rubbed it back and forth over my shoe. She did the same thing to the other one.

"Alright," she smiled, "How do you like your dancing shoes now?"

I looked. I blinked. I looked again.

"MY SHINY, RED DANCING SHOES ARE BACK!" I shouted.

I jumped off the chair and danced the Twist. "It's magic, Nen!" I said.

"No," she laughed, "just a little wash and polish."

"I love my clean, shiny, red dancing shoes,"
I giggled, spinning around and around.
Big Sister looked at Nen's big kitchen clock and said,
"We'd better get on home."
This time, I walked—I did not run.
Grandmama was shelling peas on the porch when we came back.

"Baby," she said, hugging me, "I'm so proud of you. You went all
the way to the store, and your new shoes still look beautiful!"
I looked down at my shiny red dancing shoes.
They smiled at me…again.